To Ellen Shi, who inspired me to make children's books, and to everyone with whom I've shared a warm meal of hot pot

Published by Charlesbridge
85 Main Street
Watertown, MA 02472
(617) 926-0329
www.charlesbridge.com

Library of Congress Cataloging-in-Publication Data
Names: Chen, Vincent, 1996– author, illustrator.
Title: Hot pot night! / Vincent Chen.
Description: Watertown, MA : Charlesbridge, [2020] | Summary: In this version of the
    classic Stone Soup tale, nobody in the apartment building has enough ingredients
    for dinner—so a child suggests that they have a community hot pot night. Everybody
    contributes something, bringing their diverse community together for a delicious meal.
    Includes a recipe for hot pot.
Identifiers: LCCN 2019014545 (print) | LCCN 2019020928 (ebook) |
    ISBN 9781632898937 (ebook) | ISBN 9781632898944 (ebook pdf) |
    ISBN 9781623541200 (reinforced for library use)
Subjects: LCSH: Chinese Americans—Juvenile fiction. | Sharing—Juvenile fiction. |
    One-dish meals—Juvenile fiction. | CYAC: Chinese Americans—Fiction. |
    Sharing—Fiction. | Dinners and dining—Fiction. | Youths' writings. | Youths' art.
Classification: LCC PZ7.1.C4974 (ebook) | LCC PZ7.1.C4974 Ho 2020 (print) |
    DDC [E]—dc23

Printed in China
(hc) 10 9 8 7 6 5 4 3 2 1

Illustrations done in digital media
Display type set in Cluster by Ricardo Marcin and Erica Jung of Pintassilgo Prints
Text type set in Canvas Text by Ryan Martinson of Yellow Design Studio
Color separations by Colourscan Print Co Pte Ltd, Singapore
Printed by 1010 Printing International Limited in Huizhou, Guangdong, China
Production supervision by Brian G. Walker
Designed by Sarah Richards Taylor and Jon Simeon

HOT POT NIGHT!

Vincent Chen

ꕥ Charlesbridge

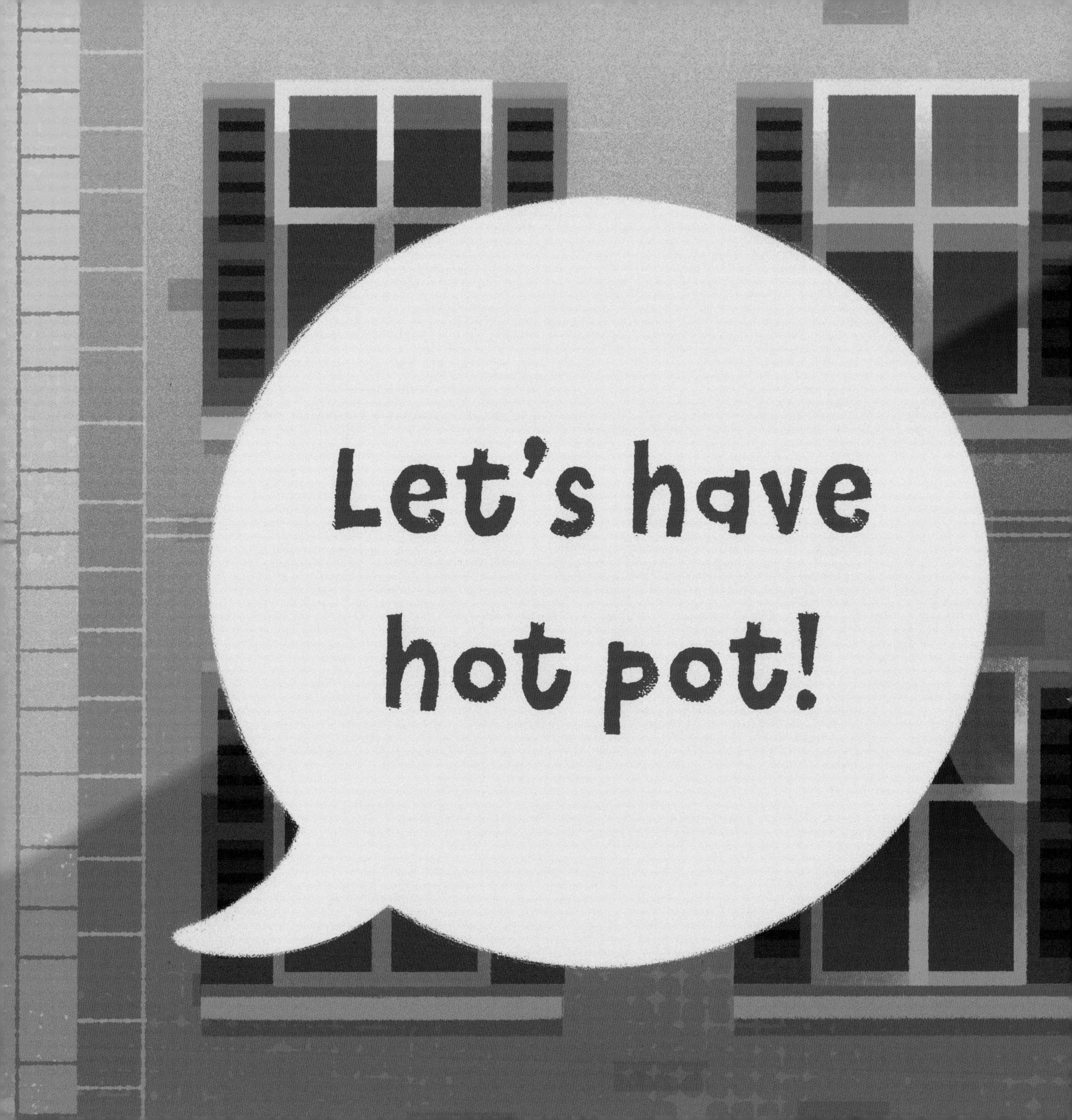
Let's have hot pot!

She brought the meat.

He grew the greens.

please pass the sauce.

Save me some meat!

There's more for all.

No more tofu.

Hot pot, hot pot!

Hits the right spot!

Hot pot is a Chinese soup that literally brings people together and encourages them to share. Diners gather around a hot pot at the dining table and add ingredients to the boiling broth. Common ingredients include meat, vegetables, tofu, noodles, mushrooms, fish balls, and more. There are many different styles of hot pot across Asia, and each family seems to have its own recipe!

HOT POT RECIPE

Here is a very simple recipe my mom taught me:

1. Chop the onion.

2. Heat up the oil in a large pot on the stove top. Lightly sauté the onion in oil until fragrant.

3. Tear about ten leaves off the cabbage and cut them into bite-sized pieces.

4. Peel the tomato and cut it into large chunks.

5. Add the cabbage and tomato to the pot and cook until tender.

6. Add the water to the pot and boil until fragrant.

7. Transfer the broth to a hot pot. (If you don't have a hot pot, you can cook all the ingredients in the pot on the stove top.)

8. Heat up the hot pot until the broth is boiling.

9. While the broth is heating up, make the dipping sauce. Everyone can mix their own to taste.

10. Once the broth is boiling, add the desired ingredients to the pot. Allow your ingredients to cook thoroughly, dip them in the sauce, eat them up, and add more to the pot!

Always cook with an adult, and be careful when using the hot pot. Use long chopsticks or small strainers to remove the ingredients, and make sure the boiling broth doesn't splash anyone!

INGREDIENTS FOR BROTH

1 yellow onion
1 tablespoon of oil
1 napa cabbage
1 beefsteak tomato
8 cups of water

SUGGESTED HOT POT INGREDIENTS

Thin slices of meat (pork, beef, lamb, chicken)
Vegetables (spinach, baby bok choy, bean sprouts, scallions)
Fish balls
Tofu
Tofu skin
Enoki mushrooms
Imitation crabmeat
Shrimp
Noodles

SUGGESTED DIPPING SAUCE INGREDIENTS

Soy sauce
Sesame oil
Sesame paste
Minced garlic
Minced ginger
Chili sauce